Jabber

The Steller's Jay

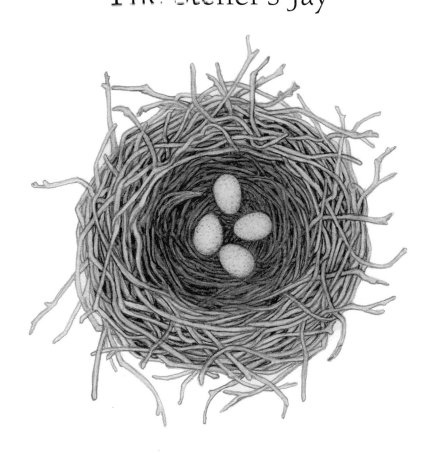

by Sylvester Allred

Illustrated by Diane Iverson

WESTWINDS
PRESS®

Library of Congress Cataloging-in-Publication Data

Names: Allred, Sylvester, 1946- author. | Iverson, Diane, illustrator.
Title: Jabber the Steller's jay / by Sylvester Allred ; illustrated by Diane
    Iverson.
Description: Portland, Oregon : WestWinds Press, [2017] | Summary: Follows a
    Steller's jay as she transforms from a helpless fledgling to an
    independent adult in the ponderosa pine forests of the American Southwest.
Identifiers: LCCN 2016034593 (print) | LCCN 2016058632 (ebook) | ISBN
    9781943328895 (hardcover) | ISBN 9781943328901 ()
Subjects: LCSH: Steller's jay--Southwest, New--Juvenile fiction. | CYAC:
    Steller's jay--Fiction. | Jays--Fiction.
Classification: LCC PZ10.3.A437 Jab 2017 (print) | LCC PZ10.3.A437 (ebook) |
    DDC [E]--dc23
LC record available at https://lccn.loc.gov/2016034593

Editor: Michelle McCann
Designer: Vicki Knapton

Published by WestWinds Press®
An imprint of

GRAPHIC ARTS
BOOKS®

P.O. Box 56118
Portland, Oregon 97238-6118
503-254-5591
www.graphicartsbooks.com

Printed in China

Jabber the Steller's Jay is dedicated to my siblings: Nina, Linda, Helen, David, Claire, and Janna. All of you have been so loving and supportive of me over the many years that we have been a family. —S. A.

To Annalyssa and CJ, two tiny naturalists. —D. I.

Acknowledgments: I'd like to thank the following individuals for their contributions to *Jabber*. Donna Nelson, my wife, for her constant support and encouragement of my writing. Jay Harrison, a colleague, made suggestions about publishing *Jabber*. Kathy Howard, acquisitions editor of Graphic Arts, read and passed the proposal forward for publication. Douglas Pfeiffer, former publishing director of Graphic Arts, was encouraging and receptive to *Jabber's* publication. Michelle McCann, editor, offered constructive suggestions and asked insightful questions while editing the book. Barbara Hawn, a good friend, suggested the name Jabber for the Steller's jay that this book is about.

Spring

Morning sun peeks over the tall sandstone rock walls, turning them a glowing red. Winter snow has melted. Tiny green shoots stretch upward, reaching for the warming sunlight. It is spring in the canyon country of the southwest.

In a tall ponderosa pine, just above the canyon rim, two Steller's jays are busy building a nest. Pine twigs and mud form the bottom and sides. Pine needles and tiny roots form the lining. Father Jay finds a puff of rabbit fur and places it inside.

Now it is ready.

The next morning four pale blue eggs with brown speckles fill the floor of the nest. For weeks, Father Jay brings pine seeds to Mother Jay, who is busy keeping the new eggs safe and warm.

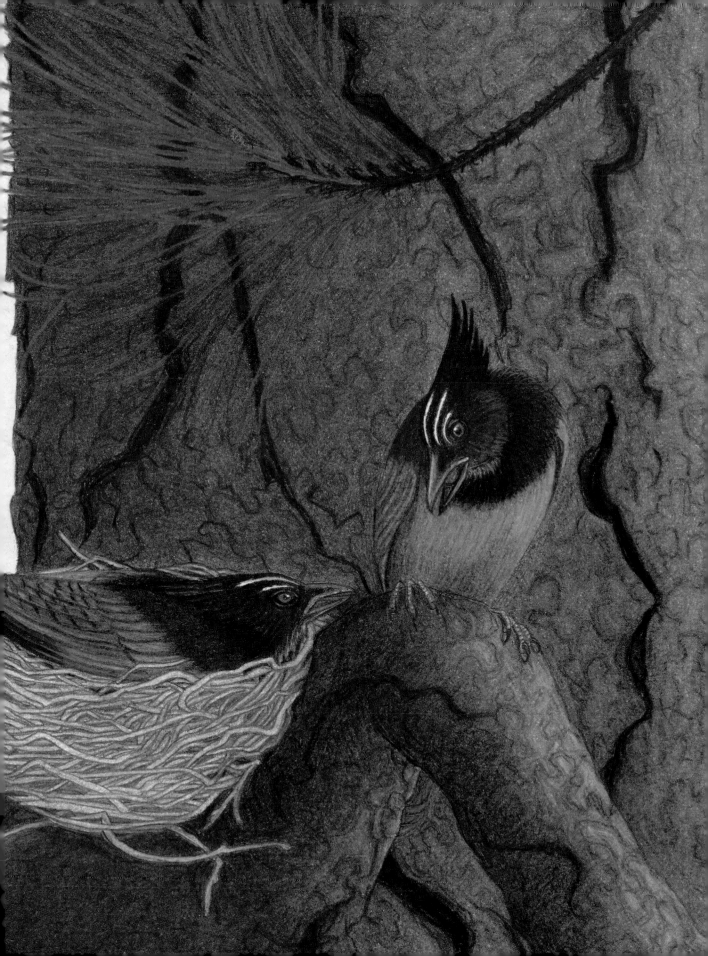

Finally small cracks appear in each of the eggs. At first nothing happens. Then tiny, sharp beaks probe the cracks, making them bigger. Slowly, slowly the shells begin to open. Four tiny babies struggle out. The warm canyon air quickly dries their wet bodies.

Now, four pink, featherless heads poke their beaks upward. Jabber and her brothers hold their beaks open for Mother and Father Jay to feed them big, fat caterpillars and tiny, crunchy ponderosa pine seeds.

Summer

The summer days are long and hot. One late afternoon a cooling rain falls. Afterward blue skies return and a refreshing wind blows through the canyon.

   The baby birds are growing fast. Soon they are covered with new blue feathers. After a month in the nest, they are ready to try their first flight! Jabber leaves the nest first and hops along a pine limb.

Leap. Flutter. Glide.

Jabber flaps her tiny wings and away she goes, landing on the limb below Father Jay, who is calling to her.

When Jabber is able to venture farther from her nest, she and her brothers explore the nearby trees. Soon, they are flying below the canyon rim where they discover a small spring.

Swoosh! Splish! Splash!

Jabber plunges her beak into the pool. She fills her mouth, tilts her head back, and swallows the cool water.

Jabber and the other jays race to a small grove of aspen trees where mule deer rest on the soft forest floor. The deer try to ignore the loud ruckus, but the shrieking jays are too much so they move away.

A red-tailed hawk soars on the warm rising air above Jabber's perch. Clouds are building. Jagged lightning bolts and booming thunderclaps echo over nearby mountains.

A summer storm is coming.

Fall

The windy days of fall kick up dust clouds, creating colorful sunrises and sunsets. Days are shorter. Nights are colder. Oak leaves turn red and yellow, aspens turn golden. Ponderosa pines drop their brown needles to become brilliantly green.

With her foot against an oak branch, Jabber holds a fat acorn and strikes it with her sharp, black beak.

Crack! Crack! Crack!

It opens. She gobbles up the seed inside and goes back for more. Jabber eats several acorn seeds then drops one. She watches a hungry chipmunk hurry away with her treasure.

She notices an acorn woodpecker stuffing an acorn into a hole in a pine tree. When the bird leaves, Jabber glides down and plucks it out, cracks it open, and eats the seed, trying not to drop this one. Another acorn woodpecker swoops down and forces Jabber to flee to another tree.

After awhile Jabber returns to the woodpecker's stash
and discovers more in its granary tree. She is wary of another
attack. She buries them in the ground beneath the brown
ponderosa pine needles for later. She doesn't notice the tassel-
eared squirrel watching her every move.

Jabber is tired, so she soars to a mighty ponderosa on the canyon rim. But she is not alone. A mountain lion rests on a large branch glaring at her with enormous yellow eyes.

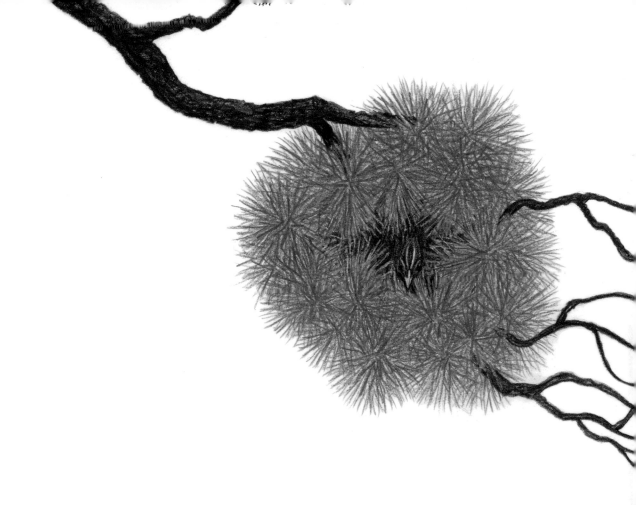

She flaps to a higher limb, then bounds up several more until she reaches a thickly gnarled witches' broom near the top. She will be safe there for the night in its tangled twigs.

By morning, a thin white layer of frost covers Jabber's wings. She stretches and fluffs her feathers. The mountain lion is gone. She is ready to start a new day.

Winter

Gray skies and heavy clouds cover the canyon country. Snow falls on the forest floor, making it hard to find food. Jabber searches the places where she hid acorns in the fall. Squirrel tracks! Her stored acorns are gone.

Pinecones have released their seeds. Oak trees have dropped their acorns. Insects are gone. Jabber is hungry and cold.

Shake. Drop. Plop!

A large clump of snow falls and lands next to her. It's a porcupine slowly making its way along a large branch above.

Jabber glides to the ground and probes the snow, sweeping her beak back and forth to get beneath it. But she finds no food there. Wet, heavy snowflakes begin to fall, forcing Jabber back to the tree for shelter. Perhaps she will not find food today.

Suddenly, she hears the calls of her flock. Together they fly through the blinding snow, searching for food and shelter from the storm. As they fly, the forest changes from the towering ponderosas to shorter pinyon trees.

The thick branches of the pinyon trees give the Steller's jays shelter. Pinyon jays fuss at them for invading their home, but Jabber fusses back. . . .

Ack! Ack! Ack!

She grabs a reddish-brown cone, pulls out a seed, and cracks the hard shell with a single sharp peck. At last, food! Jabber pulls and cracks more seeds, over and over, until she's eaten enough for the day.

When the storm passes, Jabber and her flock return to the ponderosa forest with full bellies to roost for the night.

Spring

Early morning sun peeks over the sandstone walls of the canyon, turning them a glowing red. Winter snow has melted. Tiny green shoots grow upward, reaching for the warming sunlight. Spring has returned to canyon country.

Jabber flies to the top of a ponderosa on the canyon rim. She hears a squawk as another Steller's jay joins her. The two begin to build a new nest. Soon Jabber will lay her own eggs and new baby birds will hatch. They too will learn to fly and find their own adventures in the canyons of the southwest.

Jabber's Friends

Jabber is a Steller's jay that lives in the ponderosa pine forests of the southwestern United States. Ponderosa pine forest provides many habitats and foods for the other animals that live there with Jabber. See if you can find in Jabber's story where she has interactions with the other animals.

Red-tailed hawks, as their name implies, have beautiful reddish-brown tail feathers. Their keen eyesight allows them to be always alert to rabbits and small rodents on the ground. During the day they spend many hours soaring on the warm rising air currents above the canyons.

Mule deer travel in small groups through the forest, eating grasses, leaves, and acorns. The males grow antlers, which are covered with soft velvet.

Chipmunks are very active in the spring and summer as they gather food. As soon as winter arrives they are sound asleep in their underground burrows.

Acorn woodpeckers store hundreds of acorns in holes they drill into trees, called *granary trees*. These sharp-beaked birds also eat insects they find in dead trees.

Tassel-eared squirrels spend much of their time in the trees. During the fall and winter, they grow long hairs, called *tassels*, from the tips of their ears to keep them warm.

Mountain lions are excellent tree climbers. They are predators within the ponderosa pine forest and canyons of the southwestern United States, which means they hunt and eat other animals.

Porcupines are very slow moving. They defend themselves with long stiff hairs called *quills*. They feed in the pine trees by removing bark from the limbs and trunks.

Witches' broom, while not exactly one of Jabber's animal friends, did provide shelter for her. Witches' broom is a deformity caused by a mistletoe infection, where a dense mass of pine shoots grows from a single point. These provide shelter and nests for many animals.

Pinyon jays are blue and about the size of Jabber. They form huge flocks, and eat seeds from pinyon cones and also fruit and insects.